ELIDOR
and the Golden Ball

ELIDOR
and the Golden Ball

by Georgess McHargue
Illustrated by Emanuel Schongut

DODD, MEAD & COMPANY · NEW YORK

For Georgess B.,
who read aloud
from Georgess C.,
who listened.

For Rocco
from E. S.

I

IT WAS Wales, where the boy Elidor lived, and a long time ago.

Elidor's town perched by the swift-sliding river in the valley and seemed to draw back from the high hills that stood to the north and west. The hills turned dark in the evenings and their purple shadows hid wolves and outlaws and other things it was better not to talk about. So the town did its business briskly in daytime and shut its gates at sunset. Then the flapping rooks would gaze down at the town with their yellow eyes and fly off home to tell the forest what had gone on there that day.

Elidor lived with his widowed mother in a small house

by the north gate. Although they were poor, Elidor's dead father had wished his son to learn to read and write and be an important man. So Elidor went to the school run by the monks of the nearby priory, and he might have enjoyed learning to make letters into words and words into sentences (Latin sentences, of course) if his teacher, Brother Alwyn, had not been such a harsh man. Brother Alwyn was as tall as a church tower, or so it seemed to his pupils. His voice was like stones rubbing together, his nose was like the peak of the mountain called Craig Mor, and when his hand fell on you, it was as heavy as that same rocky peak.

Brother Alwyn often beat his students, and today was one of the days when Elidor had been unlucky. Because he had stumbled over his grammar, Brother Alwyn had whipped him severely and given him twice the usual number of lines to learn for the next day.

Sore and angry, Elidor set off home from the priory, wondering what he was going to do. One thing was certain. He would never go back to the schoolroom. Never. Never. His anger made a lump inside him.

But if he were not going back to school, he couldn't go home either. Elidor saw that clearly. It was not that his mother would scold him. She would only repeat to him

what King Solomon was supposed to have said in the Bible. "The root of learning is bitter, but the fruit is sweet." Then she would add that she was sure Brother Alwyn would forgive him if he explained what had happened. As if Brother Alwyn ever forgave anyone for anything!

Elidor kicked at a stone in his path and then stopped short. In the hollow beneath the stone lay a snake—a small, silky, green snake with a pattern like gold fishnet on its scales. Elidor had never seen one like it. It stared up at him and then slid smoothly down the slope away from the track. In that instant Elidor made up his mind. He would not go home to the town at all. He would go somewhere else and live far away from everybody. He would become a holy hermit, or perhaps a fearsome outlaw. He might lose himself in the wild purple hills, but whatever happened he would never have to see Brother Alwyn again. Before he had finished thinking these thoughts, the boy's feet were already carrying him down the brushy slope.

II

Aт тне bottom of the slope Elidor came to a little
stream that sang secretly inside a curtain of trees. The sun
shone through the leaves and made a gold and green fishnet pattern on the water.

Elidor knew quite well which way he wanted to go.
Left. West. Upstream. Away from the town and the river.
It was all the same direction and led to freedom. Elidor
set off up the bank of the stream. He wanted to get a good
distance between him and the town, so he went as fast as
he could through the sweet green woods, hoping not to
meet any party of hunters or berry-pickers who might re-
port having seen him.

Elidor himself had never been in the forest before, not

even its thin, twiggy edge, and now the stream was leading him into the deep heart of it. Sometimes he thought he heard a rustle quite close by and once he was almost sure he saw a streak of green and a bright eye looking out at him from the hollow of a tree root. The sun still shone on the water, green and gold, the spring flowers were all around, and nothing larger than a bird moved in the shrubs and branches. However, a little way back from the stream the trees seemed to grow more closely together and between their strong trunks the light fell thin and blue. In fact, the whole forest was looking bluer and bluer, and the sunlight had retreated to the tops of the trees. With a start, Elidor realized that it would soon be evening, and after that it would be night. He didn't much like the idea and he knew he had been putting off considering where he was going to sleep. *If* he were going to sleep.

Elidor thought about dry, cozy caves, woodcutters' huts, and even outlaw camps with roaring fires and roasting venison, but the forest seemed empty of everything except the trees, the stream, and more trees.

Luckily, he wasn't very hungry. He had not only had his dinner in the schoolroom as usual, he had eaten a good many wild strawberries that afternoon, for the little red

fruits grew so thickly by the stream that in places it was impossible to walk without stepping on them. Nevertheless, he was becoming tired and cold, and he was alone.

If it had not been for the wolf, Elidor might never have found a place to sleep. He had just come out into a large round clearing in the trees when he heard the howl. It began like a scream, climbed up just to the edge of being a song, and then fell back into a wail that was the coldest, loneliest, *hungriest* sound anyone ever heard.

As if he had been jerked by a string, Elidor was out of the clearing and had flattened himself against the trunk of the nearest tree, a huge old oak. In another second he would have been trying to climb it, but to his astonishment he found he had pushed himself right inside the tree instead. The trunk was quite hollow.

Some other creature must also have been planning to spend the night there—for it ran off with a startled squeak. Still, Elidor was sure not even a bear could claw its way through the thick old bark, and the crack he had slipped into was much too narrow for a full-grown wolf. He scratched himself a hollow in the dry, rotted wood inside his den and fell asleep at once, like a stone sinking in a deep, clear lake.

III

Elidor was never sure whether it had been the moonlight or the singing that woke him first. He opened his eyes and saw what he thought for a moment were two huge, shining eyes staring down at him. Then he realized they were only two knotholes high up in the hollow trunk, with a rare, silver light falling through them. At the same time he felt the music, rather than hearing it—felt it through the bark of the tree where his shoulder touched it, and then through his whole body, until at last it became loud enough for his ears to notice.

He got to his knees and peered out at the clearing, which seemed to be as full of moonlight as a silver cup. Through

the forest came a group of people, accompanied by the music of harps and pipes and a drum. Men and women together, they made three circles in the clearing, one inside the other. Not a word was spoken, but all at once the circles began to move and Elidor, watching from his hiding place, knew that no one else in his lifetime had seen such a sight as this. Sweetly, lightly, joyfully, the musicians took up the dance and the dancers sang in their moving. The three circles wove into one, twined into nine, and spread into a great spiral that wound down to its center and came back to three again. The dance went on and on, never stopping, never hurrying.

Elidor had crept out of his hiding place in the tree and didn't know he had done so. He was leaning on the tree in plain sight, and didn't know it. But he did know, through his back and his fingers and the soles of his feet, that the fair folk in the clearing were not dancing alone. His tree and all the other trees in the forest, perhaps all the trees in the world, were dancing with them.

All the trees were dancing to the strangers' music and soon he, Elidor, a boy who should have been at home in bed, would also be dancing. He could no more stop himself than he could stop the stars from swinging through

the sky. He took his first step toward the bright figures. But the instant he moved, he knew he had been seen. The nearest of the dancers stopped and stared. It was a woman dressed in green and white with apple blossoms in her hair. She stretched out her hand and began to walk toward him. Then Elidor forgot the trees, forgot the dance, forgot everything about a boy named Elidor. He saw only the face of the woman, half smiling, with the huge, burning moon behind. The moon seemed to grow larger and larger while the forest, the dancers, and Elidor himself dwindled down to a tiny point in Elidor's mind, flickered like a candle flame, and then went out.

IV

WHEN Elidor awoke he found himself in a large hall filled with people, all of whom seemed to be looking at him. Dimly, he remembered being lifted down from a horse, carried inside, and set down on the floor with a thump. He got awkwardly to his feet and then the crowd parted and a woman and a man came toward him. The woman was the same one who had seen him and pointed her hand at him during the dance. The man beside her had a face that was neither old nor young. Around his forehead he wore a green and gold band clasped with a golden snake's head whose emerald eyes seemed to be watching Elidor. The man said gravely, "My name is Conor and I am the lord

20

of this place. The lady beside me is Cerridwen. Your mind has told her that your name is Elidor. But we do not yet know how you came to spy on our dancing, which is something no mortal may do. Therefore, tell us why you hid inside the great oak on the night of the midsummer moon. And I warn you to speak truly and not to lie like so many of your people, for if you do that we shall know it and things will go badly with you."

This speech astonished Elidor more than anything that had happened that day, but although he knew he ought not to anger such a great lord, he could not be afraid of anyone who looked so wise and at the same time so kind. "My lord Conor," he said, "I *was* in the oak. But I was only there because I was alone in the forest and needed a safe place to sleep. My teacher beat me and I decided to run away. I didn't mean to spy on your dance, or even hear the music. But," he added defiantly, "if I live to be two hundred I'll never be sorry I saw it, because no one dances like that in the town and because it was so beautiful and because . . . because I never knew trees could dance and now I've seen it."

Elidor didn't quite know why he had said what he did. It would have been so much easier to pretend to be frightened and sorry. But the people in the hall seemed pleased with his words. Conor reached out and drew Elidor closer to him, and only then did the boy realize that Conor and Cerridwen and all their people were very small, not much taller than Elidor himself, who was not big for his age. "That is a good answer," said Conor. "Now, Elidor-in-the-Tree, tell us whether it is your wish to stay with us and learn more of the ways of those who dance beneath the moon. You have spoken the truth to us, and truly you may stay here for as long as you do not play us false. If you choose to stay my son Bran will show you what there is to be shown in my land, the Kingdom under the Hill. Or, if you prefer to leave us, you are free to do so. Only, I warn you that once you turn your face to the upper world you will forget everything that has happened to you and all you have seen here. What then is your answer?"

Elidor did not hesitate. "I will stay," he said. "I *want* to stay and besides, I have nowhere else to go. But right now, my lord, if you don't mind, I wish I could go back to sleep. I came a long way yesterday and then I stayed up watching the dance, and oooohuh . . ." His voice trailed away in a yawn and he hardly noticed when the boy Bran led him from the hall.

Yet as he fell asleep for the third time that night, he kept repeating to himself the amazing fact he had realized when he first opened his eyes in this strange house. "I, Elidor, have been stolen away by the Faeries. Stolen by the Faeries. Just think, stolen . . . away . . ."

V

THAT was the beginning of Elidor's adventures in the land of the Faery Folk or, as they called it, the Kingdom under the Hill. Elidor had thought that was a very strange name when he heard it the night before. But the next day when his new friend Bran began to show him the other parts of the place, Elidor found out that the name was exactly true. The hall where he had first waked out of his enchanted sleep and the great house of which it was a part lay deep beneath one of the hills that could be seen from Elidor's home. But that was not all. Other houses, trees, pastures, roads, streams, bridges, and cattle were underground as well.

When Elidor first stepped outside Conor's house, he refused to believe that this was not a land like any other. He went on refusing until Bran led him to one of the many secret entrances that opened on the outside world. Then Elidor understood that the cool silver twilight that hung over the Kingdom under the Hill was completely different from the sunlight he had known. This sky, so pale and lovely, would always be the same, without snow or rain or stars or moon. He almost turned and ran away then, out into the bright, familiar sunlight that he could see at the end of the Faery tunnel. But Bran held him back and said laughingly, "I never knew one of you Human Folk before, but you certainly are as odd as they say. Why does it frighten you to find that our sky is not like your sky? After all, our cattle are not like your cattle, our dancing is not like your dancing, our food is not like your food, and our time is not like your time, either. Those things don't bother you. Besides," he added, growing more serious, "it is not as easy as it looks to leave our land by the paths to the sun. I think that if you did it too soon or too often you would get a disease of the Human Folk that is called Losing One's Mind, whatever that may be. Stay here for a while, anyway."

26

Elidor soon got over his wish to escape from the new land, although he learned that Bran was right about the many ways in which it was different from his own. The Faery Folk themselves were very small, yet there was a strange thing about them. Whenever they looked directly at him, Elidor felt that he was the one who was small, yet whenever he saw a group of Faery Folk moving in the distance he felt himself to be too large—not tall, but rough and clumsy as a bear cub in a pack of greyhounds.

The name the Faeries called themselves was the Tylwyth Teg, which meant the Fair Ones, and they had many other names such as the Silent Moving Ones, the Shadowy Folk, and the People of Peace. All the names, Elidor found, were true ones.

The Faery animals were as strange as their masters. All the Faery cattle were pure white or red with no markings and were both smaller and more graceful than ordinary cattle. So were the Faery horses smaller and fiercer than ordinary horses and their hounds leaner and swifter than other hounds. The Faeries never slaughtered their cattle for meat but lived mainly on green herbs and on saffron-flavored milk and cheese. They were not divided into nobles and common folk, but all seemed to be equal, and the women spoke first in their councils.

However, the oddest thing, the thing the boy thought most about, was the importance the Faeries placed on the truth. Now, of course Elidor had been taught that he ought to tell the truth. But from his earliest childhood he had realized that the truth was not always the safest thing to say. It was the truth that had gotten him that last beating from Brother Alwyn, in fact. He should never have said that it was Davy Thomas (Brother Alwyn's favorite) who had put the frog down his neck as he was reciting his grammar. But he *had* said it, because it was true, and so he had been beaten for lying. In the Kingdom under the Hill, Elidor suspected, no one ever made a mistake by telling the truth. Sometimes he wondered how two places could be so different from each other, but he didn't think about it very often because he had so much else to do.

Together with Bran, he went out every day to ride or swim (two things he had never learned how to do before) or explore the countryside. At first the two boys stayed under the hill, but later they began going out into the upper world and Elidor learned what Bran had meant

about the dangers of passing from one to the other. For although the way out always looked open and clear, the way in always looked like walking into solid rock or hillside. And in both directions the trip, for Elidor, was like the moment when one dives into icy water or steps out the door into a howling gale. Only, in this case, the water was icy but not cold, and the wind was howling but not loud. No matter how often Elidor did it, the trip always left him a little dizzy and breathless, although of course Bran and the other Faery Folk did it as easily as winking.

VI

THE loveliest thing that Elidor had seen in the Faery realm was a golden ball. Made of the thinnest pounded metal, it was as smooth and round and shining as a soap bubble. Of course, the Faeries had many other things made of gold. Their golden buckles, neck rings, saddle fittings, sword hilts, and drinking cups were of finest workmanship. Yet they had many objects made of wood or bronze or stone that were just as beautiful and seemed to be just as much valued.

Bran had been carrying the golden ball one day when he came looking for Elidor. "Let's play catch," suggested Elidor. But to Elidor's astonishment, Bran had never heard of playing catch. "If you don't throw a ball back and forth, why do you have a ball at all?" Elidor asked.

"You have it backward," grinned Bran. "If you want to do something as silly as tossing an object from one person to another, why use a ball? A stick or a stone or a spoon would do as well. No, a ball is only meant for one thing. A ball is to *roll*." As he spoke, he tossed the golden ball away down the path where they were standing. Like a tiny bright sun it bounded off and settled down to roll along the ground. But unlike any ball Elidor had ever seen, this one didn't wobble to a stop. It kept on rolling—over pebbles, through the tall grass, around tree trunks, and even up the ferny slopes. Bran had followed it immediately, and the golden ball set such a good pace that Elidor was almost left alone on the pathway before he shut his gaping mouth and went after them.

From then on Bran and Elidor often followed the golden ball, and each time it led to something notable or interesting. Once it took them into an abandoned mine, formerly worked by human beings. They went farther and farther through dark galleries that were lit only by the strange golden gleam of the ball, until they came to the deepest cavern of all. It was bright with fantastic crystals and in it they could still hear the groan the mountain had made when the miners tore out its treasures.

Another time they followed the ball to a clearing in the trees where a red-eyed hawk was battling a great snake in terrible silence. At first Elidor wanted the bird to win and then the snake, after he saw how badly the hawk's claws had torn it. But he could tell that Bran thought it was strange of him to want to take sides. Later Bran tried to explain. "The snake and the bird fight because they are what they are. The outcome was decided long before either your folk or mine were ever heard of. How can you wish that one should win over the other if that is not the way it is to be?" Elidor said nothing, but for many days afterward he remembered the battle and how, in the end, both creatures had been too much hurt and exhausted to do more than retreat to a tree and a hollow log.

Elidor did not always understand the things the golden ball showed them, nor did he understand that he was learning all the time—learning things that the people of the town, particularly those like Brother Alwyn, would never know or believe if they were told. Elidor was coming to understand the ways of the animals and the stones and the trees. He learned how to catch a falling star and the secrets

of the mandrake root. If anyone had asked him, he could have told where all the lost years are and even who cleft the Devil's foot. He could hear the mermaids singing, too, and he knew what tune it was that made the northern lights dance in the cold sky.

But in spite of everything that was happening to him, Elidor was still himself, of course. He was still a human being. And he was still only ten years old. It was quite natural that the day should come when Elidor began to miss his mother.

At first the boy hesitated to mention his wish to visit his home, for fear the Faery Folk might think he would betray them to the town. Yet he also knew it was as useless to keep secrets from his new friends as it would be terrifying to lie to them. Bran, it was true, could only read the most obvious thoughts of Human Folk. "It is a very great knowledge," he explained. "I shall not be old enough to learn it for several hundred years yet." However, the Faery elders, especially the Lady Cerridwen, seemed only to have to look at Elidor in order to read his thoughts as Brother Alwyn read a Latin manuscript. That was something that made Elidor a little uncomfortable about the Kingdom under the Hill, fair and friendly though it was.

One morning, therefore, Elidor approached Conor and Cerridwen and asked permission to visit his home. He was surprised that his request was granted so easily. "If you wish to go, you must go," said the Lady. "But take care, O Elidor-in-the-Tree, not to lose your heart to the People of Lies. And remember to come back to us safely and soon."

VII

Starting out cheerfully on his journey, Elidor considered Cerridwen's words. He realized that the Lord and Lady of the Faery Folk had indeed become fond of him, and that Bran would have no one else to go adventuring with while he was gone. In truth, there were very few young people among the Faeries and he now recalled that one of their names for themselves was the Vanishing Ones.

But Elidor's mind would not stay on such gloomy thoughts when he was going home to see his mother. Suddenly he began to remember the way she used to sing over her spinning, the smell of meat pies in the oven, the warmth of her arms around him, and especially all the

exciting adventures he had to tell her. How very glad she would be to see him after such a long time!

Fortunately, Elidor did not have to go nearly as far to get home as he had traveled through the forest to the Faery dancing ground. The Kingdom under the Hill had many gateways invisible to human beings, and one of them was under the riverbank a short way from the town. The boy reached his home before he knew it, bursting through the door and calling, "Mother, mother! I'm back, I came home again."

With a cry of joy, his mother dropped the pot she had been carrying and ran to hug him. Elidor saw that her eyes were red and her chin was trembling. Then she was saying over and over again, "My son, my son Elidor, where have you been? A whole day and a night in the fields alone! Oh Elidor, where have you been?"

For a few minutes Elidor was too happy to pay much attention to her words. But then something in what his mother was saying pulled him up short. *"A whole day and a night?"* Why it must have been weeks and weeks since he had kicked a stone in his path and decided to run away. How could his mother make a mistake about something so important? All in a rush, he tried to explain to her.

"I was stolen away by the Faeries, Mother. That is, first I ran away from Brother Alwyn and then the Faeries stole me. And I've been with them for weeks and weeks and they call me Elidor-in-the-Tree. They live underground but it isn't dark and yet there's no sun or moon. And they aren't at all wicked the way people say. They only want to be left alone. They were very nice to me, and I can swim like an otter and hunt like a hound. And Bran says . . ." But here Elidor came to a stop because of the expression on his mother's face.

"Oh, Elidor, how can this be? How can it be?" she asked, stepping back from him. "I think you must have lost your mind, or how could you tell your own mother such a dreadful lie?"

Elidor saw then that it would probably take him a long time to convince his mother that the Kingdom under the Hill was not just his imagination. The knowledge made him sad. He had so much wanted her to understand about Bran and Conor and Cerridwen, about the golden ball, the paths to the sun, and the midsummer dance. But how could she believe him when he himself could hear how strange the story must sound to her? And above all, how could she believe that weeks had passed since he ran

away? Suddenly he remembered the blooming roses and nesting birds that had greeted him on his way into the town that day. *It was still June in this place,* late June, just as it had been when he left home. And then he remembered something else. He remembered Bran's voice saying to him on his first day under the hill (the day that seemed so long ago, but wasn't), "Our time is not like your time." Yes, Faery time must be quite different from human time, longer and fuller and more varied. It was better time, too, thought Elidor to himself.

Once, before he had lived in the Kingdom under the Hill, he might have kept his thoughts to himself, might even have agreed with his mother that all his adventures were just make-believe. But now Elidor went and put his arms around his mother again and said firmly, "Mama, what I said about the Faeries and living under the hill was true. It was all true, and I am going back there very soon. I only wanted you not to worry about me while I was in the other place."

The rest of the day was strange for Elidor. His mother wouldn't let him out of her sight, even though she finally had to give in to his determination to return to the Faeries. She knew he was right when he pointed out that she couldn't keep him against his will. "I will just run away again as soon as I have a chance. I *have* to go back," he said.

His mother was forced to admit to herself, at least, that the boy looked well and strong. He certainly hadn't been without food while he was gone, whether it was days or weeks. And he was as neat and clean as most boys his age. He didn't look at all as if he had been sleeping out in the dirt and the wet. Nevertheless, she cooked him all his favorite dishes, honey bread and meat pies and frumenty. She also got out a clean shirt and his other jerkin for him to take back with him, even though he knew very well he could have had new clothes from the Faery Folk anytime he wished.

As soon as his mother stopped trying to persuade him not to go back to the Faeries, Elidor began to enjoy himself very much. It was good to see the familiar room, with its chests and stools and table and the iron pot hanging in the fireplace; good to hear the news of the town; good to pat the old gray dog Arva, who had belonged to his father; and especially, comfortingly good to climb the ladder to his own bed in the loft and hear his mother singing softly down below.

The next morning, however, Elidor bounced out of bed

determined to return to the Kingdom under the Hill. He intended to set off right after breakfast.

Of course his mother cried a little when he left. Elidor had known she would. But he promised to visit her again soon and at last he set off for the nearest gate to the Faery realm. Still, he hated to see his mother unhappy when there was no need. "If only there were something I could do to show her that everything is all right," he thought.

From then on, Elidor visited his mother quite often. At least, it never seemed to her to have been more than a few days between his visits, although according to Elidor's time, the time of the Kingdom under the Hill, it always felt much longer.

Elidor's mother gradually lost her fears for his safety and became used to his comings and goings. However, she never completely believed his stories and sometimes she worried that he might really be living with a band of outlaws.

One day he tried to explain to Bran about the situation at home. Before he was halfway through, however, he knew that this was one of those matters on which Faeries and Human Folk would never understand each other. Bran only looked at him with a puzzled expression and said, "You are my friend, so I am sorry you are troubled. And I know your mother is nothing but a Human Being. Nevertheless, if she would rather hear a lie about outlaws than the truth, what can you do? Come on. Let's go and get the golden ball. I feel very lucky today."

Elidor knew his friend was trying to cheer him up, so they went off together to the place where the golden ball was kept, in Conor's great hall.

VIII

THAT was the day when they met the Unicorn.

The two boys had followed the golden ball deep into a part of the forest where they had never been before. It was autumn (in the Faery realm, at least) and the silver-trunked beech trees were hung with crisp golden leaves. The leaves lay on the ground, too, and as Bran and Elidor went on it became harder and harder to see the ball rolling ahead of them. The woods had grown strangely silent and all around them was nothing but silver trees and the silver twilight of the Kingdom under the Hill. They came to a clearing and stopped still. "I can't see the ball," said Elidor uncertainly. "Neither can I," Bran admitted. He added

48

in a lower tone, "Don't talk. Something's going to happen. Can't you feel it?"

For as long as it would take to count one hundred they stood silent in the woods. Then there was a gleam of gold at the edge of the trees and without a rustle the golden ball rolled into the clearing, followed by a Unicorn.

The Unicorn was as white as the moon and its sharp spiral horn glowed like a moon-path on dark water. Too terrible to look at and too wonderful to turn away from— that was how Elidor remembered it afterward. He was afraid that the Unicorn would run off if he moved, but Bran gave a cry of delight and walked straight toward the creature. "O Unicorn!" he said with awe. "It is many years, my lord, since you honored us with a visit."

Elidor made a great effort and overcame his astonishment. He followed after Bran and slowly, slowly, the Unicorn came to meet them. When they were face to face, it lowered its head to Bran so that he could scratch the curling silver forelock and the base of the pearly horn. Elidor himself did not quite dare to touch the Unicorn, but he saw that it was watching him with its great dark eyes. It seemed to him that some secret was passing between them. Then the Unicorn lifted its head, tossed its mane once, and

49

disappeared back into the forest as quickly and silently as it had come.

Bran picked up the golden ball and the two boys set off for home in silence. In a little while, however, Elidor could no longer contain his questions. "I thought," he began stumblingly, "I thought a Unicorn would only come near a maiden, a beautiful young girl. In the town they say that the hunters hide in the forest and when the Unicorn comes up to the maiden they rush out and kill it and steal its horn, which is a cure for every sort of poison."

Bran looked at him with a horrified expression. "They do *that*? But how could even Human Folk be so cruel and stupid? Sometimes I wonder why you want to have anything to do with them at all. If the only Human Folk who can attract a Unicorn are young girls, it just shows how hard it is to find anybody but liars in your world. You see, in ancient days, when the only people in the world were Faery Folk, there were many Unicorns and they were gentle and friendly to everyone. But the Unicorn is a wise beast. It can tell what is true from what is false, and it runs away from those who do not speak the truth. Like us, it has retreated under the hollow hills and is seldom seen in the upper world. Now there are hardly any Unicorns left, and

if you Human Beings murder them so heartlessly, I can see why."

Elidor felt hurt at this reminder that he was not one of the Faery Folk. Bran saw his face and said in his direct way, "I'm sorry, Elidor. I know you are not like the rest of your people." He tossed the golden ball in the air and caught it one-handed. "Maybe you have a good idea about this game you call catch. We'll try it sometime. Come on now. I'll race you back to the great road."

IX

A FEW days after that, Elidor decided the time had come for him to visit his mother once again. Whenever he went home he hoped that *this time* he could make her believe how wise and kind the Faeries were, and how great was their magic. Now, as he got himself ready to leave, he realized that indeed he *could* take her the proof she wanted —proof that the Faery Folk were not only so rich that they had no need to steal like outlaws, but were also endowed with magical powers. He could bring her the golden ball. Then at last she would believe him. She might even visit the Kingdom under the Hill and see for herself how wise her son was to want to live there.

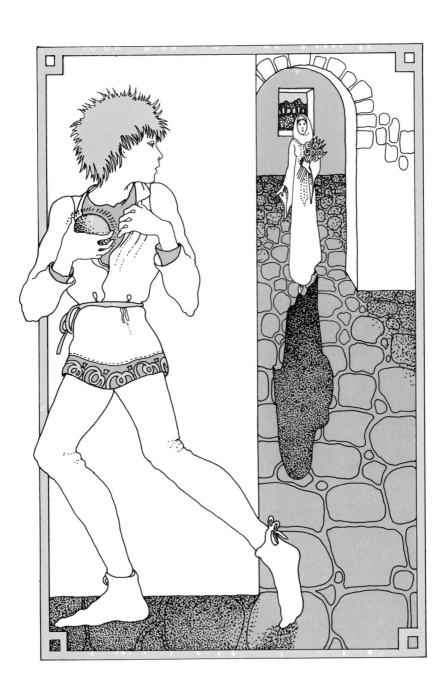

Quickly, before he could change his mind, Elidor took the ball from its usual place and hid it in his jerkin.

By this time the Faery Folk were used to his comings and goings, so no one stopped him or spoke to him on his way to the gateway that lay nearest the town.

When Elidor came out into the upper world, he saw that it was drawing toward evening, although it had been mid-morning when he started out a few moments before. Of course he knew that since the two kinds of time were different, he would find that the human world was passing through a different day and hour from the ones he had just left, but it happened that he had never before arrived outside the town so late in the day. Now he hurried along in order to reach home before the gates were shut against the dangers of the night. As he went toward the gaping gates the home-bound rooks looked down on him with their yellow eyes and jeered at him from the air. "Hurry home," they screeched. "Hurry, hurry, hurry."

Elidor began to run. He went like a deer with the hounds behind it, for the Faery Folk had taught him to move without pounding the ground like a plow horse. Through the gate and down the second street to the left he sped, and thrust open his mother's door without knocking. Lightly

56

though he ran, however, something seemed to catch at his feet as he crossed the threshold. He stumbled and fell flat, with the breath knocked out of him. Shakily, he lifted his head, and saw the golden ball roll away, gleaming in the shadows. Under the hazel bush by the front door there was a round dark hole he had never seen before. The ball rolled straight for it. Then Elidor noticed the snake curled at the mouth of the hole. It was a small, green, silky snake with a golden fishnet pattern on its scales. Like a sudden sunset the golden ball rolled past the snake and down the hole. Then Elidor heard a tiny, hissing voice inside his head.

"O Elidor, Elidor-in-the-Tree. You didn't really understand, did you? You didn't want to see that stealing is a lie like any other—the lie that says, 'What's yours is mine.' Yet, you did try, and your reasons were good ones by human standards. You cannot help being what you are. Therefore it is granted you that you will not forget what happened in the realm of the Faery Folk, though you will never go there again. So farewell, Elidor. You have chosen, and who knows? Your choice may be the right one. Farewell, farewell."

Slowly, Elidor got up and went in to his mother.

He never bothered to look for the golden ball under the hazel bush. He knew it would not be there. And he never went searching for the gates to the Kingdom under the Hill, for he understood that they were closed to him.

X

MANY years afterward, when Elidor was a grown man, he became a priest and a scholar just as his father had wished. He learned to read Latin as well or better than Brother Alwyn and he was greatly respected for his knowledge of the trees and stars and animals.

One day a famous traveler named Gerald of Wales came to the place where Elidor was living, and Elidor told him the story of a boy who had run away from school and lived with the Faery Folk. Gerald wrote the story down in a book about his journey through Wales, and that is how we know it today.

As for Elidor, he lived a long and happy life. The people of the country loved him because he understood what it was to be human. They always said of him, "Oh, you can't help telling the truth to Father Elidor. He just looks right inside you and knows when you want to tell a lie."

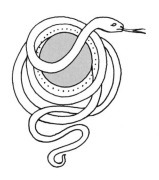

GEORGESS MCHARGUE is a free-lance writer with a special interest in myth, magic, and strange happenings. Author of seven previous children's books, she lives in Cambridge, Massachusetts, and likes to spend her leisure time poking around Bronze Age ruins in Europe or riding horseback in the Rocky Mountains.

EMANUEL SCHONGUT received his B.F.A. and M.F.A. degrees from Pratt Institute and later studied at the Art Students League and the Pratt Graphic Arts Center. He has designed many book jackets, and his illustrations have appeared in *New York* magazine as well as in other children's books.